SHIMMER

Copyright

Title book: Shimmer

Author book: Richard Alan Meredith

Text copyright © Richard Alan Meredith, 2018

Illustrations copyright © Callum Meredith, 2018

Shimmer is dedicated to my wife, Sam, who keeps lifting my chin up to remind me where the stars are.

Chapter 1: Moving Day

I stare up and through the sunroof for the whole journey. I figure that if I don't look where we are going then perhaps it won't happen. I also kid myself that it will be impossible to cry if I constantly look up. Moving house is just the next in a series of reasons why my life is pants.

You would have thought that Mum would have been going out of her way to make me happy after what had happened lately. Instead she announces out of the blue that we have to leave home (where all my smiley memories are) and go and live in a strange house, in a strange town. Moving house is the poo icing on a triple poo flavoured cake.

The sunroof view changes as we travel. It starts with a bright blue sky with wisps of white and some lamppost shaped silhouettes slowly going past. Next the frame of the sunroof is edged by tree branches which move past too fast to pick up any details. After a while the trees disappear and the sky catches up with my mood and is filled with dark and thunderous clouds, although the rain never comes. The light goes out of the day and as the car starts to make more frequent turns the lampposts return but this time they are shining down yellow light which provide no warmth.

The car comes to a halt a little too fast and the back of my head becomes unfastened from the headrest so I involuntarily take my first look at the new house.

"We're here Lyla!" says Mum with an enthusiasm which doesn't feel genuine or shared.

"We're here Lyla!" were the only words spoken for the entire journey.

I don't know how Mum knew it was the right house as it is just a large black shape against a slightly less dark sky. The street lights are broken at this end of the cul-de-sac. Maybe Mum knew this was the right house as it is the only one in the close with no lights on.

Mum leads the way to a small gate which she bumps into before opening. A small path cuts through the front garden which steps upwards twice which Mum demonstrates well is impossible to see in the dark. She also drops the house keys when we reach the front door which, without the aid of a security light, are extremely difficult to find. Since negotiating the gate Mum has hissed a number of special words. Some of which I had not heard before and all of which I am sure I would get into trouble if I repeated them. As well as being naughty words the curses did appear to have some echolocation properties as, after a particularly long combination, she finds the keys. There is more fumbling to find the lock and after some more echolocation she inserts the key and the door opens inwards.

Luckily for my innocent ears there is a light switch near the inside of the door and Mum's language returns to a 'Universal' rating.

The first thing you notice when you enter a house is not the way it looks but the way it smells. The only exception to this is your own home unless you have been away on holiday (check it out, it's true). Although Mum says... insists this new house is our home, it isn't. Home is two hours back down the road. I can smell this house and I am not coming back from holiday so this isn't home. It smells wrong.

On the left there is a set of stairs which after thirteen steps turns to the right and is swallowed by the darkness. To the right there is a door and at the end of the hall there is another door.

"Right," says Mum breaking the silence. "You must be hungry. I'll get the kitchen bags from the car and make you a peanut butter sandwich."

In as few words as possible I reply, "I'm not hungry." Despite the long journey this is true. My anger that this ridiculous idea is still stuttering forwards against my wishes is a very fulfilling meal. Maybe it could be the new fad diet, the 'Fury Diet'. I could make millions.

Undeterred by my hunger strike she continues, "Well, I'll make you one anyway. In case you change your mind. The kitchen is straight on. You can put the kettle on for me."

"Yes Mum. Of course Mum. I don't mind exploring the creepy house on my own. Anything for you Mummy dearest. I know you would do anything to make me happy." I don't really say that. Apparently this arrangement of words in this context would be determined to be sarcasm. In my experience parents don't like it when their children are sarcastic. Instead, I just think it, roll my eyes and maintain my policy of saying as little as possible to her to make sure my feelings are still crystal clear. Oh, I did huff but I don't think a huff counts as a word.

The kitchen is covered in a black murkiness. For all I know I was on the edge of a never ending black hole and when I step forwards I will fall for all eternity. That would teach Mum a lesson for bringing me here against my will, against all sense. In reality I am not keen on exacting that level of revenge on my Mum. So mostly out of self preservation I do not step off the precipice. I stay on the known solid floor of the hall, feel around on the wall just inside the door, find a switch and turn it on.

It is a bog standard kitchen with worktops, a fridge-freezer, cooker, sink, kettle and a breakfast bar. On the back wall of the kitchen there is a window and a back door, which presumably opens out onto a garden although it is currently too dark to see.

Then I notice something which really gets my interest and makes me forget myself.

"Mum! Mum! There's a cat flap!"

"Great. Can you make sure it's locked. I don't want some stray cat coming in and making this house a home."

"I would." I whisper.

I go to bed early so I don't have to put any effort into not talking to Mum. I lay on the bed staring up through a curtain less window at a blurry full moon. I weep quietly to avoid alerting my Mum. I am still too angry to give her an opportunity to make things right.

It all went full glitch when Mum and I had our first meal (does peanut butter sandwiches and milk qualify as a meal?). We were sat at the breakfast bar overlooking the back door with the cat flap. I asked Mum whether she had ever had a pet, maybe a cat?

"I did once, when I was a girl but younger than you are. Your Grandad came home from work one day with a kitten. I had nagged Dad for ages but it was still a complete surprise! She was gorgeous. She was white with patches of ginger and brilliant green eyes. Her fur was unbelievably soft and she loved fusses although she didn't really like being picked up. We called her Ginger Nut because of her patches and she used to go crazy when we got her to chase a feather tied to a piece of string. Dad said that Ginger Nut belonged to me and my sister (Aunty Helen). He said that the cat was our responsibility and between the two of us we had to make sure that she was fed and did her business in the garden. We both promised with angelic smiles that we would. Trouble was Aunty Helen and I used to argue like cats & dogs when we were kids. If there were fifty identical marbles in a bag we would fight over the one which was in the other's hand. It's what siblings do. Unfortunately we could not agree a ceasefire for the sake of Ginger Nut. We would disagree about whose turn it was to feed her and let her out. After Dad found the cat mewing for a missing a meal one too many times and after a couple of 'accidents' he warned us that we couldn't keep her and that he would find another home for her with two little girls who would look after her properly. Things came to a head when Ginger Nut wee'd on Dad's clean work clothes. He was furious. He stormed out of the house with the cat under his arm. We never saw her again. We found out afterwards that our next door neighbour had said he knew where he could get rid of her and Dad, fuelled by anger, quickly took him up on his offer. I believe Dad was telling the truth when he said he thought that Jim (our neighbour) had meant he knew where he could find her a new home. In fact what Jim meant was that he knew where to get rid of a cat with the aid of sack and some suitably heavy stones. I was heartbroken. I must have cried nonstop for a whole week. Dad must have felt really bad as he offered to buy us a new cat. But I didn't want a replacement. I wanted Ginger Nut. When I think back on it, it still makes me sick to my stomach. I couldn't go through loosing another pet again. It would be too upsetting."

I was shocked.

"Did Jim go to prison?"

"No love he didn't. It was a different time. It wasn't exactly accepted but more common. There was a time cats were just rat and mice catchers. Once they were too old and slow to catch mice they were... err... replaced."

"Mum, don't you see? This is our chance to get our own cat. We can look after it and make sure nothing bad ever happens to her."

"Lyla, you can't stop bad things from happening."

"Please Mum. She would be company for both of us and I've got no friends here."

"No Lyla."

"Mum, come on. Please. If you are worried about the extra work then I could do it. Litter trays, food..."

"I said no Lyla."

"You owe me a cat, Mum. Especially after what happened to Dad..."

Our voices had slowly been getting louder but Mum hit the highest number of decibels when she screamed, "We are not getting a cat! We are never getting a cat! I am not losing anymore loved ones!"

Chapter 2: Night Visitor

Exhausted, I pass out fully clothed. I wake in the early hours. Although physically spent my mind is clearly not. It is eager to reboot me at 3 a.m. so it can replay yesterday's disastrous pitch for a pet cat. I don't want to be awake. I want the escape of a dreamless slumber. It is as if a fairy has stolen my eyelids making it impossible to complete step one of sleep, i.e. close my eyes.

Deprived of what I want instead I get what I don't want. All of my sad face memories on repeat. As soon as I am able to eject one rubbish thought it is replaced by another equally pants one or worse: Dad dying; Mum shutting down; fighting at school; moving; yesterday evening's argument; Dad dying... I lose count of how many times I loop round back to Dad but it must be in the high teens when the silence of the house is broken by the distinctive click clack of the cat flap opening & closing.

Mum may not want a cat but maybe a cat wants us. I am immediately excited.

I sit upright trying to pick up any further noises. It's so quiet you can hear the silence. It's almost loud. I pivot on my bum and carefully place my feet on the floor. I ease myself off the bed and tiptoe onto the landing. A quick sound check... still nothing to indicate that there is a cat downstairs. Regardless, cats are stealthy. A mouse only realises there is a cat once it is breathing hot Felix breath down their neck. I try peering over the banister and back around into the kitchen. My eyes are well adjusted to the dim light although from this vantage point I can't see much of the kitchen. I confirm the hall is cat free and the living room door is shut.

I creep down the stairs trying to emulate the cat. I certainly do not want to wake Mum and have to explain what I am doing. More importantly I don't want to startle and scare away the cat. It's cold down here and I am thankful that I fell asleep in my clothes otherwise this would have been a barefoot nightie affair. I use my ninja skills to reach the open kitchen door. I poke my head slowly in.

Oh my ice cream sundaes! It's like entering a walk in freezer. It must be ten degrees colder again in the kitchen although there are no windows open. I scan the floor visible this side of the breakfast bar. Even the work surfaces and cupboard tops reveal no cat.

I reach the breakfast bar and peer over. Nothing but not a conclusive view. It must be there. I lower myself down onto my bum and shuffle along the floor. If I can make myself smaller maybe I can avoid scaring the cat away. I round the breakfast bar with another bum shuffle.

I am dumbfounded. I crawl on all fours and inspect each dark corner of the floor.

No cat.

I engage Sherlock mode and try to puzzle this thing out. Let's test my assumptions. I assumed I was awake when the cat flap opened for the first time. What if I was asleep when the cat entered and what I heard was it leaving? That must have been what happened.

I smile at myself and at the thought that I will meet my moggy soon but just not tonight. After all, us arriving had not put her off visiting.

I sit cross legged on the floor directly in front of the cat flap. The thought of pushing it open to hear the swish clack one more time tickles me so I reach forward. The door of the cat flap doesn't budge. It's locked, the same as it has been ever since Mum fastened it five minutes after we arrived.

Chapter 3: First Day at School

I'd like to report that my first day at school was a rip roaring success. I'd like to say that I made loads of great new friends and that moving was the best decision ever. I'd also like to say that my painful traverse down 'Poo Street' is over and I have turned left up 'Happiness Avenue'. I can't say any of these things because they would be lies, and I am not a liar.

Although Mum won't talk about it, I am pretty sure that me getting in trouble at school was one of main reasons we moved. After Dad died I could split the kids in school into two distinct camps. There were kids who liked me but had no idea what to say to me so generally said nothing at all. Then there were the kids (the minority I grant you) who saw this cataclysmic event as a good stick to beat me with.

"I think your Dad walked in front of that van because he couldn't face the thought of coming home from work and having to look at his disgusting mistake of a daughter, who didn't even have the guts to end her own miserable existence."

An acrid rake of a girl with short scraggy hair called Sarah Schweinsteiger said that to me. She had blocked my way while I was trying to get to the library. She lent forward until her face was about thirty centimetres from mine trying to incite a reaction. I think she wanted me to cry. Behind her four of her cronies sniggered whilst they formed an effective blockade.

Let me pause this beautiful scene and allow me to take a moment to overwrite the "Pig keeper's" version of history with a truer account.

On an average Wednesday my Dad took his usual route to work. He had parked his car and was about to cross a zebra crossing so he could catch the 7.45 a.m. train to London Bridge. He looked both ways and then took two steps into the road. He was hit by a white van travelling at approximately 42 mph. At the moment of impact the driver was texting on his mobile phone. My Dad died instantly. At 7.15 a.m., that Wednesday, my Dad kissed the top of my head while I ate a bowl of Rice Krispies and said he would see me later. At teatime (my Mum had planned a spaghetti bolognaise) he never came home. Unlike me my Dad was a liar.

One thing I have recently learnt about strong emotions is that if you don't let them out in a healthy way then they make their own organic way out. A bit like how a volcano works.

The "Pig" (I am not going to waste anymore ink spelling her full name) had made two big mistakes. One, she had completely misjudged what my reaction would be. And two, she left her chin exposed. I know I landed that first punch cleanly but to be honest, after that, the rest was a bit of a blur.

I was taken to a small room I had never been in before. My Mum was called. She came and took me home. We didn't talk about what happened but she did start cleaning the house for the second time that day.

Mum's genius plan of "new school, new start" had some merit. It was a shame it was undermined by some do-gooding teachers. We moved at least one hundred miles from our real home and what happened to Dad (although tragic) did not warrant more than local newsworthy. Therefore, my new classmates should have had no idea what baggage I travelled with. However, like a patient moving to a new ward, my old school helpfully sent my new school some notes about me and my recent troubles. A person with common sense would have come to the conclusion that children can be very mean (the evidence was clearly documented in the notes) and therefore it would be best not to give them any ammunition. In my experience precious few teachers have common sense. Those that do possess this rare quality have managed to escape an extremely effective screening process. I wasn't there (so I can't be sure) but I imagine that in morning registration (the day before I arrived) the form teacher (Miss Well Intentioned) announced to the class that a new girl called Lyla was starting tomorrow and that her Dad had died recently so we should make an effort to be super nice to her and make her feel welcome. A bully usually has to put in, at least, a little bit of elbow grease to ascertain whether a girl is weakened by Kryptonite. Without setting foot on school grounds I had a target painted on my back and short pointy things were then sharpened.

So fast forward a day (first day at school) I stand in front of 2F and get appraised. I fail to pay adequate attention to the five pairs of predatory eyes belonging to the girls sat at the back of the class.

It's a new (to me) school which I am not familiar with therefore getting lost on my way to the toilet I manage to find myself cornered in a dead end of a building by the Witches of East Preston. The only escape door helpfully locked.

I smile to myself at the photocopy quality of the scene before me as well as how quickly I have returned here despite my Mum's best intentions. What did Dad used to say? The road to hell is paved with good intentions.

This time I have the pleasure of Francine Bullock. An apt name. She is every centimetre as tall as the "Pig" but twice as wide. Why don't little kids ever pick on me? She stands with her hands on her considerable hips, legs apart with her head slightly on one side as she passes judgement on why my Dad dying was my fault and why hadn't I done the decent thing and joined him in the afterlife. Frankly used her considerable intelligence to force two neurons together and come up with her version of my Dad's demise. I am pretty sure exhaust fumes had not been the cause of death despite my personal concerns about air pollution. Despite the differences in the tale I could have sworn that she had received personal tuition from the "Pig" on bullying technique. Maybe it's some sort of bullying exchange programme. Behind her the witches cackle.

I look to the floor trying to hide my smile. Again my emotion is misread this time by Frankly (talks) Bull(ock). She interprets the bow of my head as a sign of deference, that she has the upper hand and so she moves in closer so her killer, well crafted words are clearly heard and not wasted.

I charge forward beating the "Bull" at her own game. The crown of my head connects with Frankly's nose, there is a crunch, a lot of blood, most of which ends up in my hair (Yuk!). I get taken to a room remarkably similar to the one in my old school. They can't put me in the nurse's room because Frankly is there. My mum is called again, she comes and takes me home. With no mention of what happened at school that day (parents are usually keen to talk about first day's at school) she gets the vacuum cleaner out of the cupboard under the stairs.

That night I have a dream. I would go as far to say that it was a strange dream but aren't they all? Mum and I are in the house. I am on the sofa playing my tablet but I can't get an internet connection. My Mum is pacing the living room floor carrying a new born baby crying loud enough to make me wince. As she reaches the end of the room she tuts at her failure to console the infant, turns and repeats the process. I am still trying to get the tablet to connect when I realise my Mum has stopped walking up and down and is now standing over me.

"What?" I ask.

"There," she replies passing me the wailing baby, "I can't get through to her. You try."

I wake up with a start. Not so much startled by the dream but by the fact that I can still hear a baby crying.

This noise is coming from the other side of my closed bedroom door. I slip off the bed and walk towards the door not one hundred percent trusting what I am hearing. How can the video of a dream end and the audio carry on in the real world?

I reach the door and my hand hesitates hovering over the door handle. The crying is unmistakable in its volume but it is not as frequent as it was in the dream and the sound has a bit more bass in it.

That's not a baby, that's a cat! I remember the sound from a sleepover at Seren's house back home. What was the cat's name? White Nose, Brown Nose? Something like that. Seren's cat kept mewling until we let her in the bedroom. I had better let this cat in before it wakes Mum up.

I open the door mid cry and the sound cuts out. Confused I peer around the door, open just a few inches, and then open it completely. The landing is completely empty.

Chapter 4: Lyla's Day Off

The next day I don't go to school. Apparently I can't go back to school until I seek professional advice from a counsellor. In a hand delivered letter received from the Head Teacher, Mrs. Harrington, it states that I 'have anger control issues' and 'an inability to express my feelings in a healthy manner'. Furthermore, it says I am 'unable to resolve conflict without resorting to violence' and finally I am 'clearly still burdened with negative emotions brought about by grief and the suddenness of Dad's death'. Do you think!#??

I have strong doubts that Mrs. Harrington penned a similar letter for Francine's parents stating that she 'should show more compassion to her fellow classmates', that 'a kind word can go a long way' and despite an adage to the contrary 'words can have a greater impact than sticks and stones'. Maybe Frankly should not return to school until she seeks advice from a professional bodyguard.

I awake at first light but I pretend to be asleep until I hear Mum leave for work. She leaves me a note on the breakfast bar saying that there is leftover lasagne in the fridge, to help myself for lunch and that she will be back at five to make tea. We all know what promises that I will be back at teatime are worth.

Lyla's day off. What to do? Misappropriate my best friend's car and head into the city for a day of fun & frolics? I haven't got a best friend so that crashes that app. I had better find something to do around here.

I had not properly seen the back garden in daylight yet. We arrived at night and the next day I started at my wonderful new school. The garden is a bit of a disappointment. A box without a lid sided by nondescript wooden fence panels. The only sign of life (or colour) is a square (slightly overgrown) lawn but not wild enough so that anything interesting grows amongst the grass. The only point of interest in the garden is a shed, painted in dark brown and peeling in the bottom corners of the slats. It sits in the far right corner of the space. It promises a lot as the door is secured with a large padlock. The key is not hard to find as it is on the same key ring as the back door key. With a bit of persuasion the key turns in the lock and the shackle releases.

I open the door, simmering with anticipation, to find... nothing! The shed is empty apart from an old lawnmower. Even the spiders have deserted this barren place. If I was of a mind to get into my Mum's good books I would have mowed the lawn. However, I had no intention of making that kind of grand gesture so I shut the shed door and head back to the house.

Last night's dream must have been prophetic because I really couldn't get an internet connection. I phone BT on a number I found on the back of the router but they refuse to speak to me because I am not the account holder. I try phoning a second time taking my voice down an octave pretending to be Mum.

This initially is more successful until I get to the security questions, "The name of your first pet?" I could remember the whole tragic tale in full detail apart from the cat's name. 'Hobnob'? 'Brandy Snap'? I even try 'Jaffa Cake'. After a polite goodbye I hang up the cordless phone and put it back into the base station. I then pick it up again and shout the new echolocation phrases I learnt from Mum at the dial tone and then slam the handset back into the base unit. I would have to wait until Mum came home to sort it out. This would also mean that I would have to converse with her. Maybe I'll write her a note instead.

It's amazing how much time you can waste going nowhere. It is lunchtime already and I realise I am starving. I retrieve the leftover lasagne from the fridge and warm it up in the microwave. The microwave avoids being run over by the lawnmower by doing what it was supposed to do and heating my meal with no issues.

An episode of Bargain Hunt and an empty plate later I am ready for some more exploring. The downstairs does not offer much (apart from the previously discovered cat flap) so I head upstairs. I pause on the landing, assessing where to go next. Looking for divine inspiration I look up and discover the loft hatch.

I find a hook on a pole in an integral cupboard between Mum's bedroom door and mine. I hook the eye of the hatch and open it, then pull down the metal ladder. A quick search of the kitchen drawers and I find a small LED torch. I slip it into the back pocket of my jeans and start ascending the rungs.

The mouth of the loft swallows my top half. Limited light is provided from under the eaves but it is not enough to see well. I reach for the torch, press the switch with my thumb and use the circle of light to begin my search.

At first glance the attic appears to provide the same result as the shed, not much. Rafters, insulation, roofing felt, a brick wall with rough pointing at the far end. I was about to give it up as another bust when a shadow is thrown onto the brick wall by a cardboard box.

I perch on the edge of the opening, lower legs dangling, torch in mouth so I could have two hands free to open the box on my lap. I push the flaps to the side and transfer the torch to my left hand to avoid an inevitable open mouth dribble.

The inside of the box appears to be cushioned inside (a bit Dr. Strange!). There are two small bowls. Pictures of cartoon cats on one of these indicate these are cat bowls. A water one and a food one presumably. That would make the over the top packaging a cat bed then. I pull out the snug bed and discover some sheets of paper.

The first is an A3 sheet of plain white paper. Glued onto the middle of the page is a photo of a gorgeous tabby cat. She (she looks like a girl to me) has black tiger stripes running from her front left leg, right down her body and along her tail which is curled up around her back left leg. Her chest and nose are brilliant white. She's staring directly at the camera with ethereal blue reflective eyes. The look on her face seems to be saying, "How could you wake me up!" Or 'How dare you deem yourself worthy to take my photograph!" She looks regal and powerful, like a queen.

In neat bold text at the top of the page is written, "MISSING CAT!" In smaller writing it continues, "Shimmer, our loved and very much missed cat, went missing Friday 24th February 1984" and lastly underneath the photo, "If you have any information please contact Beth Taylor, 87 Heath Close, Tel: 694251. Reward of £100 if found." Underneath this there are multiple black and white photocopy flyers of the master copy.

Stuck in the folds of the bottom of the box there is an A4 sheet of lined paper folded in half. Intrigued I retrieve and open it. It reads as follows:

The Cat in the Moon

It was a Friday when our cat went to the moon,
She was young, full of fun, and she went far too soon.

The moon is made of cheese you see,
And where there is cheese there are mice,
This makes the moon a cat nirvana,
When you are an expert mouse hunter,
With jaws like a vice.

The moon has another benefit,
It looks down on our house,
So while the Cat in the Moon dines on mouse,
She can watch over her family,
Who miss her very much.

By Beth Taylor - aged 12
20th September 1984

Chapter 5: The Plan

I wake up early again the next day. I have a plan and I am super excited to put it into action. First though, I needed to get rid of Mum. I hear her making clinking noises in the kitchen. It is clearly important to leave the kitchen spotless before she leaves for work. Well I would be highly unlikely to clean it despite finding myself with an excess of free time. Maybe she has a point.

As soon as I hear the click of the front door latch shut I am on my feet and on my way downstairs two at a time. It sounds as if wildebeest are migrating from the bedroom to the kitchen.

Bowl, Alpen, Milk, Spoon, mouth. Somehow the bowl survives being slammed down onto the breakfast bar and there is a streak of milky muesli across the worktop surface where I poured in the milk too fast. After smashing the world record for eating a bowl of cereal, I attempt two more record attempts for time taken to get dressed and time taken to brush your teeth.

I stampede down the stairs again, grab my keys and I am out of the front door. I am not one hundred percent where I am going but I am pretty sure that I spied a corner shop nearby. On the car journey to school I spent most of my time staring out of the window taking great interest in everything so I avoided any chitty chat with Mum. I was mostly bored but the shop, and the potential to buy sweets, got my attention. At this moment I wish my parents didn't have a 'no smart phone' policy and I could have GPS'ed my way there. As it is I would have to use 'The Force' and hope I remember my way back.

I resist the urge to flat out run and power walk to the end of the cul-de-sac. Left and right look identical, pairs of semi-detached houses on both sides of the road. I can see a T-Junction terminating the road to the left but not the right where the end of the road is eaten by the horizon. I don't remember which way Mum had turned toward school. On the gamble I will get to the Seven Eleven quicker I turn left. Reader, I do understand that this way may not be quicker if I have set off in the wrong direction.

I reach the corner of St Cuthmans Road and if I didn't know better I would have sworn I had walked in a complete circle. Pairs of semi-detached houses as far as the eye could see in either direction. I turn right this time and cross the road. I pass a few further options on my right but they offer similar views. The road bends round to the right twice and then comes to an end at another T-Junction albeit this one has a set of traffic lights. I feel like I have been trekking for Mordor and my frustration grows as my plan appears to be unravelling as well as the risk that if I walk much further I may struggle to find my way back.

I spot an old lady on the other side of the road. Her short wavy hair is completely grey, she is wearing thick lensed glasses and it is clear she has a quite few layers under her already warm

24

looking coat even though the weather is quite mild. She is tottering forward, her stoop looking like it is providing some forward momentum whilst she pulls one of those shopping bags on wheels that only people of a certain age seem to have. Maybe these wheeled contraptions are presents from the Queen on your hundredth birthday.

I wait for a gap in the traffic then run across the road. In my haste I keep running until I am only a few steps away. I don't think her frail body is capable of jumping but her whole body goes into a coordinated spasm at my surprise materialisation. At these closer quarters I notice the hearing aid in her left ear.

Semi recovered she eyes me suspiciously. I don't help matters as my eyes keep wandering to her roller bag. I'm thinking she knows where the shops are and she's thinking I am assessing whether her purse is in the shopping cart. The media has a lot to answer for.

"Hi!" I try to sound bright, friendly and unthreatening.

"Shouldn't you be in school?" she says warily.

"No, it's OK. I got kicked out." Too much honesty, not helping.

She's looking more concerned now so I try lying instead.

"I've just moved into Heath Close and I wanted to go to the shops for Mum because she works all day and it's only me and her now."

It took a moment for her to register what I said (maybe the hearing aid causes a delay like a long distance phone call) but then she manages a half smile and the tension appears to release from her small body.

She points back the way she has come. "Down that way dear. 1st right. Follow the road to the end then left and the shops are across the road on your right."

"Thanks!" I shout over my shoulder as I sprint off powered by excitement.

The shops are exactly where my guide told me they would be. There is a parade including a bakers, a hair dressers and, what I was looking for, a Seven Eleven.

I sweep in and the magazine and newspaper pages open in my wake. It's hard to find things in a Seven Eleven. In a supermarket baked beans take up metres of shelf space and there are tens of different kinds. In a Seven Eleven there is not much shelf space and the tiny partition for the beans is inexplicably next to the crisps, dog food and bleach. A tasty combination! In my haste I don't find what I am looking for on the first circuit of the shop. I slow down for the second lap and half way down aisle two I find what I am looking for. From the bottom shelf a black & white cat smiles up at me.

There is more choice than I imagined possible: Junior; Adult &; Senior. I had never seen our friendly neighbourhood cat so how did I know? On the theory this cat is probably eating out of bins I decide it probably doesn't matter. Adult is half price and I am on a limited pocket money budget so decide to go for that but which flavours? It's a straight choice between chicken & beef or fish. Beef seems a strange choice for a domestic cat who could never even dream of taking down even a calf let alone a fully grown cow so I go for fish. All cats like fish. I wonder if the supermarket has more cat appropriate flavours like 'Rat' or 'Mouse'? Once I had Mum on side I would find out.

I take the box of foil sealed pouches to the checkout where again I am eyed suspiciously by the man behind the counter. His face relaxes when I say I am out shopping for Mum who is not well (I am not entirely sure that last bit is a lie). I pay with loose change but am affronted that I have a pay 5p for a carrier bag. Do they want me to use this establishment as my preferred cat food supplier or not?

The bag feels very flimsy so I don't risk running home. Out of the shop I turn right instead of left and therefore do a poor job retracing my steps. Luck is on my side as the end of this road (St Cuthberts Rd) adjoins St Cuthmans Rd which is where I started. I had clearly taken the long route to the shops.

I get back to the house to find the front door open. I must have done that. I did leave the house in a rush. Well as long as the house has not been stripped clean of its valuables (I am thinking the tablet, blu ray player and the TV) then the 'no harm, no foul' rule kicks in as well as 'what Mum doesn't know can't hurt her'. On cue Mum emerges from the kitchen carrying my box of cat treasures from the attic.

I decide that the best course of action is to lead the conversation and put Mum on the back foot. My mouth opens and closes like a tuna as my mind draws a complete blank.

Mum gives me time to compose my thoughts. She stares at me and I can feel anger radiating out of her in waves. The harder I think the more barren my mind scape becomes. After an uncomfortably long silence I feebly manage, "Hi! You're back early."

"Where have you been?"

"To the shops." Too honest!

For the first time since she appeared from the kitchen her seemingly unblinking eyes move from mine to the bag in my right hand. It's a quick glance then her eyes lock onto mine again.

"Did you go to the shops to pick up the bits I needed?"

I blurt out "yes" clinging onto a slither of hope there is some escape from this confrontation.

"Don't lie to me Lyla!" she thunders sounding like she is shouting in my ear rather than being at the other end of the hall.

In an unnerving manner she recovers from over boiling and returns to an intense simmer.

"And what's this?" she asks inclining her head toward the box.

Trying to be vague but still honest I say quietly, "I found it in the attic."

"Why would a little girl (a bit condescending but in the circumstances I feel it best to let it pass) hide a cat bed and bowls in her room and then sneak off to the shops and buy cat food when she has been expressly told that getting a cat is as likely as your Dad walking in the front door and asking, 'What's for tea?'"

Damn these biodegradable carrier bags, she can see right through it!

"And why do I keep finding the cat flap unlocked despite locking it every time I go past it?"

Although I had bent the truth to breaking point a lot that day I am honest when I say, "That wasn't me."

I am aware enough to know it sounds like a lie and I brace myself for another ear drum shattering blast. Instead (and more worryingly) she transfers the cardboard box to her right hand only, crushing its side to get a grip. Then, with frightening speed, she strides toward me with a face constructed of pure fury. Now I am not easily frightened (as you have previously seen) but I root to the spot frozen.

Neither of my parents believe in corporal punishment and as a result I have never been smacked. Even when I ruined Uncle John's new fitted kitchen by painting it red with a tin of paint I found in the shed, I escaped unscathed. Regardless of this knowledge I am now convinced I have pushed my Mum too far and she is going to administer justice with her newly freed left hand or, less likely, the box. I half close my eyes and turn my head away as she reaches me.

I completely misjudge it. She streaks past but in one fluid movement wrenches the carrier bag out of my grasp.

I hear a lot of echolocation words (ELW's) although my Mum should not need them in the daylight.

"I am going to throw this ELW in the ELW bin. No more Lyla. I can't cope with anymore ELW from you."

I hear her throw the stuff in the car, she slams the car door shut and speeds off like a police car in hot pursuit.

I stand there numb and defeated with my back to the world and my head down. It takes a long time before I turn and shut the front door behind me.

Chapter 6: Shimmer

Mum comes back at teatime. The fire and brimstone in her eyes has gone out and she just looks tired and sad.

We go through the motions: tea; TV and; escape for us both at bedtime. We don't speak a word to each other all evening. There is a huge barrier between us and neither has the energy to fight or right it.

I lie in bed hoping sleep will take me. Although my heart is anaesthetised, my mind is wired. I stare at the ceiling and watch the shadows of the tree branches shudder in the wind.

I don't hear the locked cat flap open and close. My subconscious barely registers the first meow echoing from downstairs although the one outside my bedroom door is loud and impossible to ignore. I turn my head to the side. An electric blue light bleeds into the room from the bottom half of the gap between the door and its frame.

"What the..."

I slip out of bed and approach the door. Not sure what to do next. Another noisy meow makes me jump. The desire not to wake Mum overrides all and I open the door.

The whole of the landing is bathed in fluorescent blue light. The source of the light is a small cat. It looks up at me, tilts its head to one side and almost looks like its saying, "Thank you!" It saunters past me, inspects the room, then with an effortless jump, lands on my bed. It turns a half circle to face me and makes itself comfy with its paws tucked up under its chest. It stares straight at me with a look which seems to say, "Come on then. Hurry up! Give me a fuss." I shut the door, turning the handle to be as quiet as possible. I then make my way slowly back to the bed. All the while the cat never takes its eyes off me but shows no sign of fear. I kneel on the floor so we are on the same level. The cat continues to stare at me invitingly. Her face is only 30 centimetres from mine and it is unmistakeable. It's Shimmer! Although she has all the same markings as the photo (white nose, white chest, etc.) it's the eyes and imperious look which distinguishes her. The difference now is the ethereal blue which permeates from every hair on her body like impossibly bright fibre optics. This can't be happening. Cats don't live for 34 years. Plus they definitely do not glow bright blue!

I can't take my eyes away from her. From this distance I can hear the deep resonance of her purring. She continues to wait patiently, still purring but keeping me transfixed with her sapphire eyes.

I reach out my hand to fuss her although I am not convinced she has any substance at all and that my hand will pass right through her.

Shimmer can't resist following my hand and looks upward to the ceiling to offer me the side of her neck. I feel a hum of electricity as we almost touch and I hear a voice say clearly, "Beth, it's me! I came home!"

The voice shocks me as I don't hear it with my ears. The voice echoes loudly, directly inside my mind. As a result I move my hand away.

Shimmer looks at me accusingly and continues, "I've travelled a long way for this. Where's my fuss?!"

I lower my hand again and Shimmer raises herself up to meet me. The electrical hum gets stronger as we get closer, my fingers begin to tingle and the hairs on the back of my hand stand up on their end. I make contact with her impossibly soft fur then everything goes white.

I must have closed my eyes in reaction to the brilliant white light. I open them but find myself on the bed instead of the floor. Maybe Shimmer was a dream. A very intensely blue dream.

The room looks different. The window, door and integral wardrobe are in the same positions but the neutral beige carpet has been replaced with a bright multicoloured weave, the magnolia walls have been painted orange with a textured wallpaper underneath and the bed is covered with blankets rather than my 4.5 tog duvet. There are unfamiliar posters on the wall. I find the lettering hard to read. Either I have sleeps still in my eyes or I need an eye test. The Police? Nick Kershaw? Lookin Magazine? What's Lookin Magazine?

I am laid down on my tummy which is a bit strange because I always sleep on my back. I push myself up and jump off the bed.

Never mind my eyes, I have bigger (or more to the point) smaller problems. I am stood on the floor but looking up at everything including the bed. I must be only 30 centimetres tall. Am I still dreaming? Have I drifted into a psychosis to escape my miserable reality or has that electric blue cat put some serious whammy on me?

I walk over to the wardrobe as it has a mirror door from top to bottom. It takes longer than usual having the gait of a Power Ranger action figure. Maybe I have been turned into a toy!

Even though I had considered the possibility I might be a magically animated toy I am still stunned by my reflection. I'm a cat! I'm Shimmer!

Eventually I remember to breath. The smell is so intense it feels like it is being pumped up my nose, inflating my head and then escaping out of my ears. The smell is down the slope of the roller-coaster wonderful. The bedroom is pungent with the warm and heavenly scent of Beth. Oh I love Beth! I wonder where she's gone. Maybe she's gone to find me some food. I know! I'll bet she will be in the kitchen.

I gracefully descend the stairs and announce my arrival into the kitchen with a loud meow. I can still smell Beth but the smell is fainter. She's not here! And to add insult to injury there is no food in my bowl either.

No matter. It's time I did my rounds anyway and with a swish-clack I am out through the cat flap and into the garden. I open my mouth so I can take in the full spectrum of smells. Basically check out what is going down.

Oscar! I hate that cat! He's been in my garden again. I trot over to the corner of the shed where he marked his scent. Yep, definitely his foul stench and only a few hours since. He must have been in the garden while I was asleep. Well he had better hope I am asleep next time otherwise I will show him what happens to trespassers!

A flash of movement down the side of the shed catches my eye. I am downwind and the smell is unmistakable. Rat! Lunch on the run. Just what I was smelling for.

I scamper down the side of the shed and the rat (who had frozen when it had realised it had caught my attention) takes off and disappears under the fence. Too narrow for me so I go up and over landing in the flower bed the other side. Dinner thinking it was safe under a leafy canopy breaks cover and sprints across the lawn to the bins at the side of next door's house. I run too following the scent trail. Man this is fun!

The pursuee scurries under the side gate and again I go up and over hoping to pounce on the other side. It's fast food though and I just miss it's scaly black tail with my Roland killer paws.

The rat must have thought that was too close as well because it panicked and jumped into the back of a van parked on the drive. Checkmate rat, you're cornered!

I make the easy leap into the van and stop. I don't want the rat to slip past me. The van is full of boxes so plenty of places to hide. I peer around the boxes on the left and the right but no sign of the rat. Rats are tasty but not stupid. Take the left route and he escapes to the right, take the right and he escapes to the left. Rats are clever but cats are cleverer. I won't do either.

I silently jump onto the nearest box and creep stealthily across the top. I do a quick scan of the floor before I move onto the next box. It's dark in the back of this van which is to my advantage. A few boxes in and I spot a huddled brown form breathing quickly near the back corner of the van. I move carefully into position, body and chin low. I am so close now I can hear my prey's rapid heartbeat. In my nervous excitement my whole body quivers, my pelvis moves from side to side and my tail moves like it has a rattle on the end of it. I try not to make these involuntarily body movements and the rat hears them rotating its ears in my direction. It's too late, I'm too close, I pounce, death from above, rat for breakfast. I am so caught up in the moment I fail to notice the lights go out as the van doors close.

Chapter 7: Lost

I don't know if it was the stress of being locked in, or the motion sickness, but the rat didn't stay in my stomach for very long.

Beth has complimented me on the loudness of my meow on many occasions (including the early hours of the morning) however no-one hears my wails of, "Let me out!" over the guttural roars of the engine. Eventually, horse and exhausted, I fall asleep.

I am awakened with a start by a loud bang when the van jumps into the air. The box I am lying on lands back on the floor and then slides forward colliding with the inside wall of the van. The movement ends and the engine dies. I hear the driver door open and slam shut. The footsteps move toward the back of the van. I coil myself ready to spring in anticipation of the rear doors being opened. Poised, I wait and I wait and I wait some more. The door remains shut and I don't hear any more noises outside. Eventually I slowly stand up and let out a quiet and morose meow.

I think I am in hell. I lose track of the number of times I am woken by the van stopping, the driver getting out and thinking this time the van's rear doors will open. At first my hope is close to stratospheric at the thought that this time I will escape and be reunited with Beth. However, the height my hope falls from gets lower each time we stop as the result is the same. Even my famously loud meow deserts me. I open my mouth and cry silently into the darkness.

It must be morning because the sunlight wakes me up. I yawn and stretch right through to the tips of my razor sharp, rodent killing claws. I can't feel the softness of Beth's blanket and I can't smell her either. All I can smell is rat. It's not unusual for me to bring Beth a rat as a present. I've never seen her eat them but she must love rat because she never leaves me any leftovers. This rat though smells like it is decomposing and partially digested. I hear a deep voice. I struggle to see in the brightness (did I mention I see much better in the dark?) although my eyes adjust enough to see a blurry silhouette of a man. He is waving his hands back and forth in front of his face.

My confused brain suddenly untangles itself. I am not in Beth's room, I am still in the back of that van! But this is the chance I have been waiting for. Paw's don't fail me now!

Humans don't see so well in the dark and the man jumps back in surprise when I streak past. It is also possible he thinks I am a super-fast zombie rat. That would scare even me!

After spending so long in the gloom I am blinded by the daylight. I keep running in a straight line over rough and gravelly ground until the sound of the horn from a large truck blasts and I change direction. Within a few strides I find myself on softer ground surrounded by tall grass. Heart racing but feeling more secure under cover I stop and try to gather my bearings. A sniff close to the ground doesn't tell me much so I brave raising my head above the grass and taste the breeze. My mind goes into overload at all the new smells. None of them are familiar and no sign of Beth. I'm lost!

Chapter 8: Into the woods

I stay hidden in the grass next to a type of human meeting place I have never seen before. All day long (well between napping) I watch humans leave in their cars and vans via a very wide, and impossibly fast, road. They pull up next to some metal boxes where they appear to feed their shiny beasts with hoses pressed to a small hidden mouth near the rear end of the vehicles. Weird! Afterwards the humans enter a nearby building to get some food for themselves before re-joining the blur road.

When the sun goes down the number of vehicles stopping begins to peter out until eventually none stop at all and one last human leaves the building and, after the lights go out, he leaves in his own metallic steed. Only then do I dare to venture out from my hiding place. I have a raging thirst so I try to sniff out some water. My olfactory sense leads me back across the gravel patch to the side of the human building. I know a puddle of water is nearby but I can't see it. Well water is see through after all! I don't know how humans see it with their rubbish eyesight. I suppose every animal must have its own superpower. I tentatively reach forward with my paw. It breaks the surface of the water and the ripples catch the limited light from the road. I plant both my front paws into the water before I lose sight of it and lap up a very long drink.

As soon as I quench my thirst my stomach growls reminding me it requires prey as well as water. I don't need my super powered cat senses to smell out some food. A few metres away, at the back of the human building, are some of my favourite human invention... Bins! From a nearby concrete platform I dive straight in. It is super-sized compared to our neighbour's one back home so it takes me a little longer than usual to find what I am looking for. A beef burger complete apart from one human sized bite. Humans are weird throwing out perfectly good flesh. This burger even came with bonus protein rich maggots!

Fed (comfortably full actually) and watered my mind focusses on my next priority, getting back to Beth. Food and water were easy enough to find. They were close by and not much of a challenge for my enhanced snout. With no familiar smells my nose is useless to provide a clue as to which way to go.

I walk around to the far side of the human building. I see the slip road where the vehicles were leaving the blur road and stopping for a feed. This would have been the way I arrived in the back of that cursed van. I can't retrace my steps. Cars that are too fast to see mean certain death. Even if there was a chance of survival the smell of the road is too much to bear. The blur road twists and turns off into the distance like a slow worm. It's banked on either side by a thick, green forest. I may not be able to trace the edge of the road closely but there is another option which may be even quicker, walk a straight line through the trees.

In the distance the trees don't look that big but up close I realise they are gigantic. To get round the trunk is a short walk. I crane my neck and come to the conclusion that these must be the trees which hold up the sky. Beth could never get me down from those. Cats aren't scared of the dark (including the lightless forest - our eyesight is too good) but when the trees are that huge you start to wonder how big the animals which live in it are. And what they like to eat!

I yawn, stretch and sharpen my claws on the bark of the nearest tree. I look back at the blur road. Certain death versus a good chance of being eaten by a giant forest monster? I close my eyes imagining Beth and my heart aches so badly I almost cry out. I peer as far as I can into the deep, dark wood. If I can be stealthy enough to catch a rat (and they have super hearing) then I can be stealthy enough to avoid being a midnight snack. Staying low I tiptoe into and through the undergrowth of the trees. Put some food in my bowl Beth, I'm coming home! Beyond the tree line I am swallowed by the dark and disappear from sight.

Chapter 9: In the woods

I don't think I have mentioned this before, but my eyesight is phenomenal. Add to that my nose and my super stealth and you have a lean, mean, rat killing machine. Having said that, at home there is always some source of illumination: a street lamp; a house with the lights on; even a full moon. This forest of the giants had next to none. I suspect it is a cloudy night although I can't see the sky through the thick canopy provided by the trees. There isn't a breath of wind either. The net result is that whether I rely on my eyes, nose or both I can only sense a couple of cat lengths in front of me.

One thing which appears to be working very effectively is the one superpower I didn't realise I had, my internal compass. It feels like it is a part of my heart and it pulls in Beth's direction and me along with it. It would have me going twice my current speed and crashing through the undergrowth but I don't want to advertise 'Free Lunch'. Luckily my pragmatic head keeps it in check as I carefully pick my way through the bracken and brambles always one hundred percent sure that I am heading in the right direction.

At the car feeding station all I could hear was the blur road. Now that I am deep in the woods I can't hear the road at all. Not that it is quiet though. The forest is noisy. I can hear small animals rustling through the undergrowth. This noise is comforting when I start to consider where my next meal is going to come from. I can't imagine any human prize bins in this much nature. More worryingly I can hear the occasional snap of larger twigs. A sound that only can be made by bigger animals. Bigger animals than me. Well at least if I can hear them they are not hunting. I know it's the predator you can see, or hear, which you don't need to worry about. For the first time in my life I understand what it feels like to be the rat! Beth, I wish you were with me.

I can also hear owls high up in the enormous trees. I don't usually worry about owls. Back home we have an unspoken agreement that I am rodent death from the ground and they are rodent death from above. It's to both of our advantages that mice and rats have their attentions divided between the ground and the sky. Monstrous trees may mean monster owls. Death from above may come for me too. I would be the joke of the neighbourhood, the cat who was killed by a bird. I try to rotate my left ear to listen for sounds from behind and above.

The only thing I am confident about in this pitch dark and dangerous world is there is no death from below. I stop dead in my tracks facing an entrance to a tunnel leading underground. The opening is tall and wide enough for me to comfortably fit through, and it stinks. It stinks of a dog. No not dog... fox. It seems inconceivable that the residual smell of a fox could smell quite so bad. I am right. A long, whiskery muzzle pokes out of the hole and the black, wet nostrils open & close as it sniffs the air. The rest of the face follows and I suddenly find myself nose to nose with a very large and angry fox.

Chapter 10: Death from below

This isn't the first fox I have met and although never friendly we usually agree to disagree. With their large mouths full of white knives I believe a fox is more than capable of despatching a cat (respect). However we cats have formidable weapons with our killer claws and equally sharp teeth. Foxes also recognise this (respect). So usually after some circling, hissing, bearing of teeth and an occasional (claws unsheathed) paw swipe we go our separate ways with an occasional look back just to make sure that the other party does not take the opportunity to pounce on the other's back. That being said I would have thought that this fox, seeing danger right outside its front door, would have retreated back into its home allowing me to pass by unmolested. What you want and what you get are clearly two distinctly different things. I should have learnt that by now.

Foxy Loxy pauses as the smell of city cat hits its nose. The shape of the fox's mouth develops into a snarl revealing the dangerous teeth. My ears vibrate in response to the fox's low growl which sounds like an idling engine. With precision placed footing the fox slowly exits its hole with its eyes locked onto mine. In fear, I back away from the hole and give it room to fully exit. In retrospect I should have flashed a warning strike with my paw there and then and, once it had retreated into its tunnel, made a break for it.

The face is indicative of the fox's overall size and it towers over me at first before crouching low (defending its neck), teeth still on show, large bushy tail in the air and a look of pure fury in its eyes. Recovering my nerve I answer the challenge in kind. I open my mouth fully showing all my teeth, making it very plain about the consequences of coming any closer. I flatten my ears and make all my hair stand on end in an effort to look bigger. Heedless to any other dangers in the forest I let out a high pitched yowl. Eyes still locked we begin circling in the fight dance. It's in the fight dance where we assess our enemy's weaknesses, our chances of victory and escape.

Why is this fox being so aggressive? Why didn't it take the safe option and retreat back into its hole? It must have known I would not have followed and predators are nothing if not practical. We rarely bite off more than we can safely kill and chew. We make half circles before returning the way we have come. The fox always keeping her back toward the tunnel entrance. Suddenly it all makes sense. Two fox cubs peer out of the hole to see what all the noise is about. Mothers are fearless and will defend their cubs against animals a lot bigger than me. I'm in a lot of trouble.

I'm no threat to her young ones but she doesn't know that. All she knows is that there is a potential cub killer sniffing around right outside her home. I could play submissive, show that I am not a threat, but I am not convinced that this wild dog can speak cat body language and wouldn't just take her chance to eliminate me.

We keep half circling left and right, the tension heightening each time. She darts forward, snapping with those ferocious teeth, she retreats as I flash a paw full of claws at her nose. Her aggressive moves become more frequent and my timing in parrying is equal to it but I only need to make one mistake (one slip on this unfamiliar ground) and I am toast. I can't see how this can end well for either of us as she will not back down or give me room to escape.

Finally I get my chance as the braver and more curious fox cub begins to make its way out of the hole. For the first time Mother Fox's eyes leave mine, glancing back at the wayward cub. I sidestep forwards and left following through with a claw strike with catches her on the right jowl. She instinctively closes her right eye and turns her head away to the left. Taking my opportunity I make a dash for it on the fox's unsighted side. She takes a blind bite at me as I hear her jaws and teeth snap close behind me and feel some fur being pulled out of my tail.

I run and run blindly through the undergrowth until I am out of breath. I make myself small and try to listen out for any sounds indicating that I am being chased over the sound of my thumping heart. I don't hear anything I would recognise as Mother Fox in pursuit. My heart slows and, exhausted, I fall asleep deep in the thicket.

Chapter 11: The Bare Necessities

I wake up to the pleasant sound of birdsong. It must be morning as light is penetrating the forest canopy creating random patches of light across the woodland floor. I yawn, stretch and dig my fox defeating claws into the rich earth.

Illuminated the forest is a less foreboding place and with the score 'Shimmer 1, Woodland Creatures 0' I prowl off confidently in search of something to eat. I may have rediscovered my mojo but I am very tired. I could lie low waiting to pounce on some unsuspecting small animal which may wander by but I am mindful I may still be in Mother Fox's territory, not to mention the ache in my heart pulling me toward Beth.

Luckily for me I stumble into lunch not long into the day's trek. The twitter of a song bird gets my attention. I spy the small, greenish coloured bird in the nest of a nearby tree. Looks delicious! The bird not the tree! Humans have loads of names for birds but I have improved this system by simplifying these categorisations to small, medium and large. This covers all levels of hunger the bird may fulfil from slightly peckish, hungry to starving. I scale the opposite side of the trunk using my fox destroyer claws which double up as handy climbing gear. When I judge I am high enough I round the trunk to the branch supporting the nest. Keeping my head and body low I make my way slowly along the bough. A brittle piece of bark snaps as my claws dig into it. The bird's head swivels round. I've been made! It takes to the wing and taunts me by perching on a tantalisingly close branch on the tree opposite.

I stand up, now that stealth is no longer required, and notice that, despite my failure, the nest is not empty. Nestled in the twigs are three small eggs, light blue mottled with brown specks. I saunter over, can't quite believing my luck. If you can't dine on songbird then eggs are a great consolation breakfast.

I lick my lips while I decide which egg to start with when, to my surprise, the nesting bird dive bombs me nearly knocking me off the branch. I am at least 4 grown up humans high so I make myself flat gripping with my claws for dear life.

I spot Mother Bird on another nearby branch watching me. I raise my head and make eye contact. I glance down at the eggs and I am immediately forced to duck again as she whistles past my head. Every time I try to begin breakfast the result is the same. My empty stomach grumbles.

How on earth am I going to eat these eggs without personally testing how soft the woodland floor is? Cats are cleverer than birds and I have an idea. Staying flat I reach out with my left paw until my multifunctional claws get a grip on the edge of the nest and then pull. At first little happens but gradually the nest works its way loose until it takes a great fall. It almost takes me with it but I manage to retract my claws just in time. I turn and crawl back along the branch the way I have come. The bird completes a few revenge fly bys however I get to the trunk unscathed. Blooming Mothers!

I find the eggs smashed on the woodland floor. Saves me breaking them. I lap up the protein rich goodness. Satisfied, I allow my heart to lead as I continue my quest to find Beth.

Chapter 12: Forest Life

All in all I have taken to life in the forest like a cat to dry land. In fact, if Beth was here with me, I reckon I have the skills to hunt enough food to keep us both well fed.

Not having travelled before I didn't realise that they have the same food in the wild as they do in the city: mice; rats; birds; frogs... I even caught a dragonfly in mid fight and they move as fast as cars! I celebrated in style by biting its head off and swallowing it whole.

Having said that some food in the forest have their own exotic differences. Take squirrels for example. As well being a little bit smaller than their city cousins forest squirrels are red! Can you believe it, red! They still taste the same as the grey ones though, a bit nutty!

The only animal I haven't seen, which are as common as mice and birds back home, is another cat. So imagine my surprise when on the breeze I catch the distinct whiff of feline. Now there is not a cat alive I can't beat down and after the fox face off I feel invincible. This unfortunate cat is directly in the path of me getting to Beth. It is going to get a very clear message to get out of my way or suffer some clawful consequences.

The environment is starting to change. The trees are thinning out, broken up by large granite boulders. It is much colder and windier and I have never seen the clouds so close to the ground.

Even weirder events were to come. As I round a colossal stone the sun becomes completely eclipsed. Stranger still is that the smell of cat, female cat, is stronger than ever. It's then I realise I am in the shadow of the biggest cat I have ever seen.

She is the height of three of me with paws the size of my face. She has a white beard and tufts sprouting from the top of her ears. It must be a forest fashion, the squirrels have these ear tufts too. She fixes me with a stare from her cold grey eyes which would have made Mother Fox disappear back into her den and not come out until spring. This Queen of the Cats looked like it could kill a rat the size of a deer. I, on the other hand, am a cat the size of a large rabbit. In context a snack sized rabbit.

This is it. This is the end. I have successfully scrapped and beaten cats nearly twice my weight but between me versus this monster, there could only be one winner. And it's not me. My speed is legendary so I don't get hit that often but when I do, I am tough and make sure that I land multiple blows before my opponent can even attempt another swipe. If her majesty hit me even once I would be dead. If I landed a hit the best I could hope for would be to scratch one of her front legs. To get to her face I would need to reach up and expose my belly to her. Again the result would be the same, dead house cat. Powered by my foolish pride I have swaggered right into this big cat's swiping zone. If I turned and ran now I would be squashed by her impossibly large paws and despatched. Exactly how I would finish off a rat.

Caught between indecision and mortal fear I curl up into a tight ball with my head buried into my body and my tail tucked underneath. In my final moments I think of Beth and my broken promise to find her. I feel the deepest of despair that I will never feel her again and she'll never know what became of me.

I feel the Queen's breath on my neck as she moves in for the death bite. Her powerful mouth forms around the back of my neck. I imagine that I am back in Beth's bedroom, ecstatically purring as she fusses just behind my head. I await the inevitable crunch of bones, hoping for a clean kill. However the mouth closes on the scuff of my neck only and, next thing I know, I am hoisted up into the air.

Eyes still shut I swing back and forth in the big cat's mouth as she jogs across the rough terrain. I have been dangling here for quite some time. This does not make sense. If she wanted to dine on me in private then surely she would kill me first to eliminate the chance I might try to escape. As I have said before, we cats are nothing if not practical. However taking live prey home for your cubs. Now that makes sense. There are no humans out here with giant tins of cat food so a cat which doesn't learn to hunt, and kill, starves to death. After my cowardly humiliation of how easily I had been caught, I take comfort in the thought I intend to go down swiping. I may not have the weapons to bring down a queen but, against a little princess, I stood a chance.

My stomach lurches as the Queen ducks her head and I assume we are entering her den. She places me gently on a soft bed of what smells like bird feathers. I wasn't even dropped or hobbled. She is planning on giving her cubs the full live prey experience. I get my second chance to die with honour. My whole body tenses as I ready myself for the scrap of my life. I open my eyes determined to show my opponent no fear.

What I see when I open my eyes is a big surprise. The largest tongue I have ever seen is about to envelope my face with a giant lick.

Chapter 13: The Good Life

I have to admit that was the best wash of my life. Two reasons for this. Since chasing that cursed rat into the van, I haven't had much opportunity for personal grooming. Secondly, and probably more importantly, that tongue is an immense cat washer. It can groom me from the top of my head to the tip of my tail in one glorious lick.

I don't know why I was adopted although the absence of any cubs in the den explains it to some degree. However I couldn't say for sure where the cubs went. Perhaps another predator took them while the Queen was out hunting. Maybe stricken with grief she found me and adopted me as her princess. And, oh boy, was I treated like royalty.

Mealtimes became super-sized. Song birds were replaced by pheasants, rats were replaced by goats and rabbits were replaced by deer. After every meal I was close to bursting and if I didn't fall asleep there and then the post repast wash was guaranteed to send me off to sleep.

I am ashamed to say it but life was so good that I completely forgot Beth. Luckily for me Beth had not forgotten about me and she came to me in a dream.

The Queen and I are, back in the forest, hunting. We are in full on stealth mode. Every paw is precision placed, making next to no sound, to ensure that we do not reveal our presence to any potential meals. I look up at my protector, awaiting a sign she has seen something. She does not look back at me but keeps her head low, facing forward, looking and smelling for something tasty to eat. All the while we keep moving forward. I am super-charged with excitement. What is going to be on the menu today? Will it be grouse or snowshoe hare? Will it be chamois or frozen deer? Will it be pheasant? Marmot or mouse? We'll have to wait and see. It's this excitement which powers my muscles today and I feel like I could leap up and pluck a high flying bird from the sky.

The Queen freezes, stopping mid step, with one paw still off the ground. An ecstatic thrill of anticipation tingles down my neck, back and finally my tail. She's seen something although I know not what as the undergrowth blocks my view. She remains motionless for what feels like an eternity. She becomes part of the forest like a stone. I don't find it hard to play the part of inexperienced cub as I find it next to impossible not to shake with excitement.

The Queen betrays her location with a staccato look to her right and accelerates off in that direction. I tear off after her allowing my pent up nervous energy to escape through my leg muscles. I have no chance of keeping up with the long legged and powerful Queen but I feel unadulterated joy as I follow in her wake. Her trajectory of broken bracken and her scent are easy to follow even though I am sprinting at full tilt. The

Queen's path now changes from a straight line to a zigzag. A sure fire sign she has closed in on her quarry. If I see the Queen's face post prey pursuit this is always a bad sign that lunch has escaped. However she has her back to me, her rear is in the air and her short stubby tail is on show. The signs are promising.

As I get close The Queen is shielded from view behind some particularly thick and taller than me undergrowth. Her scent is strong now and I know she is on the other side of this foliage. I burst through it full of the rich, arrogant pride of the hunter however what I smell and see stops me dead in my tracks. The Queen has caught Beth and now it is her turn to be as still as stone.

I wake up with a start. I am in my usual spot in the den all cuddled up with the Queen although I feel cold from the inside out. The dream is still fresh in my nose and I suddenly don't want to be here anymore. For the first time in a long time my heart reaches out and pulls toward Beth. The Queen is asleep and I use my stealth powers to extricate myself and sneak out of the den. It's raining outside. The drops are so big and heavy that I am quickly soaked, like I have fallen into water. I hate getting wet (it's a cat thing) but I will endure anything to get back to Beth. The dream still echoes in my eyes and nose so I head out into the storm.

Chapter 14: The Long March

All warmth drained out of me after I left the Queen on that impossibly wet night. My heart is with Beth and the joy in my life I left with the Queen. I am stuck in between, any empty shell.

It's another grey day. It's been either overcast or raining ever since I left the den. I am trudging through yet another brown, ploughed field. There may be life in the soil waiting for the sun until it pops up and shows itself but for now it stays hidden. I seem to be the only living thing on this field and I am only half alive. Alive in body only.

My Beth Compass, since switching back on, feels more like a curse than a gift. At its awakening I wanted to chase it like it was a butterfly. Now it feels like a collar around my neck dragging me onward. I am so tired. What if Beth was only a dream? What if the Queen really was my Mum? If that's true then I have left my real home, plentiful food and the love of a mother to chase a dream, a phantom... I am pitifully thin. The good life all but a memory. As you know I am a ferocious and efficient hunter even if I can't always keep my food down! Hunting is joy and joy is hunting. I have no happiness left in my heart therefore no hunger for the hunt. I kill on instinct prey stupid enough to directly cross my path. Even then they might have a good chance of escape. A dragonfly hovered over my head yesterday. It may as well have been as high as the moon.

It's a good job Mother Fox is so far away. I would not pose her any challenge now.

It starts to rain again. Not as hard as before but each drop is icy cold and lingers on my fur then rolls down to my skin. I still hate the rain, despite plenty of opportunity to get used to it, and my paws have disappeared in as much furrow puddle water. I veer off the ploughed track and head towards the edge of the field to look for some cover. I find a weed with some largish leaves. I lie down under the biggest tucking my paws in under myself in an effort to keep warm and stay under its umbrella. The weight of the rain bends the leaf and I am only marginally drier than being out in the open. I no longer care. I close my eyes and sleep claims me.

I am woken by the sound of wet squelchy footsteps. I look right, toward the sound, and I can't believe my eyes. Beth is walking up the side of the field following the first furrow. She is barefoot and wearing her nightie with the strange multicoloured pony on it. I have spent quite a lot of time in the forest, and countryside, but have never seen a pony coloured like that. Her feet are covered in mud and with each step, fresh mud seeps up between her toes. She is looking at me her eyes crinkled in a smile. She is carrying something in each hand. She stops as she reaches me, blocking out the sun, which has finally returned. Her toes are so close I could lick them. Maybe I should clean them but I am too stunned to do anything except stare up at her colossal form. She squats down and places my bright orange food bowl in front of me and then empties a tin of cat food into it. It's more than she would usually give me. Maybe she thinks I need fattening up. She gives me a quick fuss and pleasure explodes inside me. She stands up and, after a final look and smile, she turns and walks back the way she has come revealing the sun which now dazzles my eyes to blindness.

My eyes finally adjust and I notice the bright blue sky. I look right but Beth has disappeared. I can't even detect her scent but I can smell something else. My food bowl has also disappeared, replaced with a dead but still warm rabbit. There are no signs of a wound or obvious indications of how the rabbit died. Maybe it wandered past, spied me and died of fright. Well I am pretty scary you know. Despite how plausible that this rabbit's heart froze when it saw me is, I don't believe that is what happened. Beth brought me this meal. I don't know how she did it, but she did. No matter how many times I fail her she never gives up on me. I fill up on tasty, juicy rabbit and then, after a doze (well I am a cat after all), I turn right to follow Beth. The sun is strong and I am now warm on the outside as well as the inside. I skip over the top of the high side of a furrow and leap, snapping a small bug out of the air. It doesn't taste very nice but it's not the point. I'm back!

Chapter 15: Smash & Grab

Now that I was looking on the brighter side of life I could see that farmland offers some obvious advantages over the forest. Fields don't plough themselves, humans do it. And wherever there are humans there is always easy food. The trick is working out how to get it. And, as you know, we cats are canny.

I am skirting the edge of yet another field when I see lights illuminating the windows of a farmhouse. I ignore the pull of my Beth Compass and take a little detour. The front of the house offers little, just a low stone wall punctuated by a gate tracking the perimeter of a small front garden. Maybe the goodies are round the back! I tiptoe around the side of the house then stop dead. I am downwind of another blasted fox! My stealth, and the wind direction, have served me well and he doesn't notice me. In fact he is heavily engaged in digging his way into a small enclosure. There could be opportunity here for the predator who uses her head rather than her brawn. There is a tree a little way behind me and to the left. In stealth mode I make myself invisible and head back to the tree. I make a super leap and land silently on an overlooking branch, camouflaged by the bushy leaves. I am hidden but have a clear line of sight to the fox and his digging activities. In fact, if I wanted to, I could pounce on him now and despatch him just like the rat in the van. Based on the smell I can't imagine that fox tastes very nice. No, I'll bide my time and see what he is up to. Some movement, and noise from the far side of the enclosure reveals what the prize is... chickens! Now I have thoroughly enjoyed the vast array of forest food I have tasted on this adventure but chicken, now there's a true taste of home.

Now I need to engage my superior cat intellect to see how to make best use of this situation. The fox has already dug a hole big enough for me to fit through. I could jump down now and startle him so he runs off. Leaving me to help myself to fresh chicken. No. That's a bad idea. There's no guarantee that my surprise arrival will chase him off and I will end up in another fight dance. As confident as I am I have to recognise who fled last time (got the last swipe in though). No. The best plan is to wait for the fox to break in, pick his chicken (after all he has done all the hard work) and leave with his take away. When I know the coast is clear I can go in and pick another. All without getting one spec of dirt under my claws.

He stops digging. He pulls his front half in and, with a bit of a wiggle and jiggle, his back end including his big brush of a tail follows. The chickens go into full panic mode and start running round the enclosure making a right old racket in the process. Stupid birds! Surely one of them would think to escape out of the hole the fox has made. The killing frenzy has consumed the fox and he is chasing down and snapping the necks of each chicken. I feel jealous and start to think that I have should have gone for Plan A. However, at that moment, I hear the dog. Scratch that, I hear dogs.

Despite dogs and foxes being cousins (I can tell by the smell) dogs hate foxes every bit as much as we cats do. Maybe dogs look down on foxes as backwards bumpkins, holding on to old ways and not realising the smart way is to work with the humans. Come to think of it cats and dogs do have quite a lot in common. It's a wonder we don't get on better. Having said that I can't even get on with next door's cat!

The dogs are beside themselves barking and howling. They must be tied up somewhere. Then I hear them on the paw. Someone has let them loose.

Mr. Fox has finished his killing spree and is now dragging his chosen chicken through the hole. I think he has left it too late though as two large and ferocious looking dogs come bounding around the side of the house. The fox spies them and flees through a hedge with the dogs hot on his tail. The chicken is still half through the hole. Tut, tut, tut Mr. Fox. All that effort and nothing to show for it.

A particularly burly human arrives on the scene. He looks down at the half posted chicken and makes a very angry noise. He's scarier than the dogs! He takes a few steps forward, puts a stick to his shoulder and... BANG! The loudest noise I have ever heard emits from the stick and a flash of light temporarily turns night into day. I almost fall out of the tree in shock but manage to cling on with my front paws although my back end and feet are dangling in the air. I right myself dragging my rear end back onto the branch. The man chases off after the fox and dogs barrelling through the hedge. I hear another blast from the thunder stick. Luckily for my ears he is some distance away now.

Plan C it is then. Ears still ringing I leap down from my perch. So easy. I retrieve the half-posted chicken. The neck does smell of fox spit but I can always eat from the other end. Chicken secured in my killer jaws, I trot off in the opposite direction to Mr. Fox who is having a decidedly bad night. Score so far, Shimmer 2, Foxes 0.

Chapter 16: The World's End

The pull of the Beth Compass grows stronger each step I take. I think this is a good sign that I am getting closer with each pawfall. The terrain changes every few full moons from farmland to forest. I know how to look after myself in both, so I stay healthy and well fed. Occasionally I come near a blur road but thankfully never have to cross the big ones. The Compass also bids me to cross streams, but I always manage to find the stone paths to keep me happily dry. In the forests when the clouds get low again, I wonder if I will encounter another giant cat like the Queen. Even big cats have stealth mode and can make themselves invisible. Maybe I have passed by one and just not known, or maybe she was the last of her kind. I hope not.

After several moons of warm weather, the wind starts to turn cold. I hope I will see Beth soon. I need her warm body to cuddle up with.

I am sure you have noticed that sometimes I look for food and sometimes food finds me. This time it is the latter. It's a chilly day and I am trekking through another wood. I am not bothering to be particularly stealthy, so I am making significant progress towards Beth. I disturb something which explodes out of the undergrowth. It's a rather unusual rabbit. It's completely white! I wonder if it will taste different to the usual grey/brown ones? Only one way to find out. Its fluffy tail bobs up and down in front of me as it attempts to put distance between me and it. I can't resist, I give chase.

I am faster than the rabbit and I think he knows it too. As soon as I get close he changes direction with little, to no, loss of speed. This is one of the few super powers I do not possess and the rabbit gains an advantage but not for long as I close the gap again. I get within a whisker of tripping the rabbit with my paw when he changes direction again. I keep up the chase, although I am not sure how long I can maintain this pace, and follow the white rabbit right through to the end of the forest. Scratch that, I mean the end of the world.

The lucky rabbit makes good on his escape, and disappears back behind the treeline, as I stare at the space where the ground should be.

My Beth Compass tries to pull me past where the ground runs out. My instinct takes control of my heart and my claws clamp into the sandy soil before my heart tries to test my flying abilities.

How can Beth be beyond the end of the world? It doesn't make any sense. After a long time of indecision some large white birds appear out of the nothingness. I've seen them type of birds before. Back home I usually chase these off and steal their lunch. They use their impressive yellow beaks to slice into bin bags. How could they have flown out of nothingness? There must be something beyond the clouds, a way to Beth?

I peer down to where the ground has fallen away. Down the sheer face there are plants growing, rocks protruding and other natural ledges. I can only see so far down before the view is swallowed by the clouds. There is a way down with all the nooks and crannies but it looks extremely dangerous. Well extremely dangerous for any creature who hasn't got the skills I have.

I have been crying out for ages.

I was making great progress down when unexpectedly a small ledge of sandy soil and grass fell away from the edge of the cliff. I started to fall with it but I instinctively reached out with my multi-purpose claws and manage to scrag onto a tough woody plant. Panic stayed with me as my rear end was dangling in free air (again!) and I feared that the plant's roots would let go and I would plummet to my doom. Perhaps scared for itself the plant held on and I was able to scramble onto a rocky crag which felt assuredly solid. I owe that plant my life. I swore to repay the debt by killing the next herbivore I come across, once I get down... or up. But I was too terrified to move. So I did the only thing left to do, I decided to cat up and cry out for help. Beth has come to my rescue before and she'll come again.

I have cried for so long now that my meow has completely dried up. Time to be practical again. I carefully peer up and down from my hiding place. I can't see any obvious way to climb up. Down though there is a similar rocky outcrop that I am on now, surrounded by similar plants which saved my tail last time. My Beth Compass is urging me to go on, not back. Some of my plant friends are there if needed and I am more than happy to repay any life debts. Feeling slightly sick I tentatively start to make my way down again.

Well isn't that just perfect!

I have reached the bottom of the cliff. I have risked my life and tail to find the scent trail runs out. The cliff ends at an impenetrable barrier. Water!

Water as far as I can see in all directions bar the cliff at my back. It's not ordinary water as it smells of fish and moves with a life of its own. It slaps the cliff below before gathering herself for another blow. Sometimes the water hits so hard that the water sprays up and threatens to make we wet too! Was that on purpose? I am very far away from purring!

What can I do now? There is no way I can go back up. That sheer face is full of booby traps and I used up most of my nine lives making it down. I could traverse along the water's edge until I find dry land but what would be the point? My Beth Compass is clearly indicating the love of my life is across the water. I use my super sight to peer across the watery expanse. Is that land I can see on the horizon? Or is that just wishful thinking. We cats can swim you know but it still doesn't change the fact that we hate getting wet. On cue the living water hits the cliff particularly hard, soaking me with it from super nose to super balancing tail. I am wet now anyway and Beth is worth a good soaking. Make sure the cat flap isn't locked Beth, here I come! With that I jump paw first into the water and start paddling.

I used to think water was flat. That's one of the reasons it is hard to see. This water is not flat, it is made up of hills which, after you get over the first one, you find out there is a bigger one on the other side. I have been catty paddling for ages now but I have no idea if I have made any progress toward land. My Beth Compass keeps telling me I am on the right flooded track so I keep pawing water.

It's dark now and I think I have made my last mistake. The living water has found a new game, hitting me. The water hills continued to get bigger and bigger until eventually they became water mountains and started to collapse. Collapsing onto me, burying me under the water. I swim hard each time and break the surface gasping for air. I am running out of cat power but the mighty water does not seem to be running out of energy or enthusiasm. I continue to be pummeled, mercilessly with rhythmic efficiency.

I just reach air before another water mountain collapses on top of me, but I succeed again and grab some precious air. This monstrous water does not know who it's dealing with! I shall never give up! I will conquer it as I have defeated all who have challenged me on this journey. Water mountain, collapse and smash! I don't reach the surface this time and everything goes black.

Chapter 17: Beach Life

Ow.

Ow!

Oww!!

I am awoken by a recurring sharp pain at the tip of my ear. My blurred eyes adjust and I can see a cloudy, grey sky and the living water moving back and forth along some sandy ground... OWWW!!!

Something is pinching my ear hard. It feels like, whatever it is, is trying to rip it completely off. I am lying on the ground and whip my head around to confront the source of the torture. In my rich and varied life I had thought I had seen it all. I am very wrong.

The first thing that is very wrong is its eyes. They are not in its head but sticking out on stalks above. And its head is not on an elegant neck (such as I have), it has no neck at all with the rest of its head squashed into its round torso. Under its eyes its small mouth is opening and closing constantly but it isn't making any noise. I might have double vision but I could swear it has more than four legs. And the hands! Great, big, oversized hands which seemed to have been specifically designed to cause me extreme pain. Let go of my ear you evil, fishy smelling demon!

I jump up and the pinchy thing (probably one of the living water's minions) finally let's go. It looked so big when I was lying down but now it is suddenly cast in my shadow.

It gives me one last appraising look, just to check I am really not dead, and then runs off sideways towards some water filled rocks. I am about to give chase to see if one of his stalky eyes would come off easier than my ear when my vision blurs up again and I throw up water. Lots and lots and of fishy tasting, salty water. The fishy smelly bug thing with the oversized hands sensibly takes the opportunity and makes good on his escape.

Still feeling queasy, exhausted and with the sorest of ears, I drag myself away from the water's edge until I reach drier sand and some tall grass which protects me somewhat from the bitter wind blowing in from the living water. I am chilled to the bone as I am still damp. I try to give myself a wash but my fur makes me extra thirsty so I stop.

What now?

I look out across the living water in the direction of my Beth compass's pull. I can't try that again Beth. It almost killed me. In fact, the only reason I am still alive is because the living water spat me out. Maybe I don't taste too good. Someone should tell the pinchy bug.

Maybe there is another way across. Maybe the living water is like a giant stream. Maybe there are giant stones where I can use my super jumping ability to get across.

It starts to rain. You'd think that being already wet on the outside and the inside would mean that I wouldn't care but I do. The nearest cover is a small cave cut into a blue grey cliff. The sand is damp but at least there are no drops of the evil stuff falling from above now. I tuck my paws under my body to reduce the amount of me in contact with the ground (an old trick as you well know by now).

The cave overlooks the living water. It's a long way out but still moving. Maybe it knows to keep its distance. Any enemy which takes the beating I did and is still not beaten demands respect. Yes, we can do the fight dance again and next time I will get past you and reach my Beth. I blink but my eyes take more time than usual to reopen. Sleep is taking me making my eyelids extra heavy. I drift off thinking of Beth, more certain than ever that when I wake I will return to her.

Chapter 18: Checkmate

I wake up in panic breathing water. I am so stupidly arrogant. The living water was keeping its distance, waiting for me to lower my guard before coming back and finishing me off. I bound for the cave entrance, the water already reaching the top of my legs. The living water has already anticipated my move and slams me back inside with a wall of water higher than my head. I am out of my depth now so switch to catty paddle power to get out. There are no walls of water to throw me back but the living water pulls at my paws instead. She let's go and I start to make progress, but any headway is mocked as she drags me back to where I started. She is playing with me. She knows she can let me go for a bit because she can grab me again whenever she likes. I can't really complain, how many times have I toyed with my prey?

The roof of the cave is getting closer now as it slowly fills with water. There is no rushing this, the living water is enjoying herself. I dive down trying in vain to find a way out at the back. There is none or at least none that I can find. I break the surface of the water at speed desperate for breath and bang the top of my head on the ceiling of the cave. The shock of the impact causes me to stop swimming and I sink momentarily before instinct forces to paddle up again for air.

And the water keeps mercilessly pouring in. My bruised head is being rubbed against the ceiling and the water is now up to my chin. This my last chance. I take a deep breath and dive. I aim for the blurry light emanating from the cave entrance. I make progress and then I am pulled back. I keep paddling with all my cat might and the living water loses track of me as I surge forwards through the brine. I am going to make it. My muscles start to slow as my body craves essential air. You can have air once I get to that light! Keep going! My body tries to take a breath even though I know I am still underwater. I start breathing in water in fits and starts as I fight my body's instincts. My paws and legs are flailing but not in any coordinated useful way. Then I stop fighting. The need for air disappears and is replaced with an all-encompassing calmness. My super smell and hearing have deserted me (even the Beth compass has gone quiet) but I can still see the blurry light of the cave entrance. It starts to slowly darken. Maybe the sun is getting low? Eventually it all turns black apart from a tiny blue light dancing in the dark.

Chapter 19: Home

I open my eyes and find myself in front in the wardrobe mirror at Heath Close. I stare back at myself wide eyed, there in body but not in mind, not fully conscious, not comprehending. Lyla, what just happened?

I start to replay my recent memories which are clearly not mine, they're Shimmers'. It all felt too real and the experience too long to have been a dream. I have been a cat, a lost cat, for months and months. Shimmer shared everything with me. Her experiences, her thoughts, her feelings, her hopes and dreams, even her death.

As if to confirm, "Yes. That did just happen," Shimmer meows at me. Sat just to the right of me she looks up with that contented look on her face, "Hi Beth!" She is not visible in the reflection of the mirror but her iridescent blue glow explains why I can see myself in the pitch dark as I have now been stripped of my cat super eyesight. She continues to stare enraptured and then blasts out another happy meow, "Beth! We're home!"

"Yes Shimmer, I think you're right. We are home."

Shimmer gives me one last pupil dilated look before she turns and nonchalantly struts out of the ajar door onto the landing. I can still see her iridescence penetrate around the door frame. Maybe she wants food? But what do you feed an incorporeal cat? Ghost mice? Humans find it hard enough to catch the live ones. An empty tin of Felix? Maybe Mum would go for that. A cat that doesn't cost anything and can't die because it's already dead.

I follow her out onto the landing and to my surprise she is sat waiting for me, directly outside Mum's bedroom door. Still with the same loving look on her face she lets out another trademark, high decibel meow, "Bye Beth!" The edges of her shine start to peel inwards and her radiance intensifies as her form begins to shrink. Her outline continues to implode until all that is left is a tiny pinprick of intense blue light which dances up and down along the landing towards the stairs. It does not make it that far before winking out of sight.

A familiar groggy voice calls from behind the door.

"Lyla?"

Mum.

"Is that you?"

I open the door and tiptoe in. Shimmer has already woken her and yet it seems impolite to stomp into her room.

"Yes Mum. It's me."

I can just make out that she has propped herself up on her elbow although her face in this light is unreadable.

"It's the middle of the night. What's wrong?"

"I... I... had a bad dream... Can I sleep with you?"

I think I can detect a smile but I can't be sure.

"Of course you can hon," and she throws open the duvet to invite me in.

I cover the distance with a run then a dive and she wraps me up in a strong cuddle before sealing me in under the covers.

"I'm sorry Mum." The word 'Mum' comes out higher than normal and I start to shudder as emotion takes hold causing tears to pour uncontrollably from my eyes.

Mum slowly fusses my hair and kisses the top of my head. I feel moisture on my forehead when she says, "Me too hon, me too."

Congratulations for finding *Shimmer*!

Beth would be overjoyed to hear from you with news of her beloved cat.

Go to
www.foundshimmer.com
to claim your reward.